Ollie the Otter With Riley and Oscar

by

Garth Tuxford

I hope you enjoy my Children's tale.

Ollie the Otter

With Riley and Oscar

By

Garth Tuxford

ISBN: 9798574586716

Independently published

Ollie the Otter.

"Oh, this is good, the sun has come out and I do like the sunshine. Now all I need is a friend to play with."

"Mommy told me not to go too far on my own she says there are too many enemies of the otter out near the river, but I cannot see any."

"Still, I had better keep my eyes open just in case something bad is close by."

"Hey, hey are there any friends out there who would like to come and play with me?"

"This is my first time out to play on my own and this is going to be so much fun."

"Oh, who is that over there cooey, do you want to play?"

"Oh dear he doesn't look very friendly; I hope he isn't hungry."

"Hello Mr Fox, I am only little, please don't eat me."

"Grrr Why don't you come a little bit closer and I will play with you?"

"Not likely my mom warned me about foxes, I'm off. Catch me if you can."

"I want to find someone who is little and wants to be my friend, I must see if I can find someone."

"Who is that splish splashing just down here? I wonder if it is another otter like me."

"Oh, this is good it's a little boy, I wonder if he would like to play."

"Hello little boy, what is your name, and would you like to play?"

"I'm Riley, who are you?"

"I'm Ollie and I need a friend."
"You won't bite me, will you?" asks Ollie.

"Not as long as you don't bite me." says Riley.

"Alright that's good, we can be friends then."

"Do you live in the water like me?" asks Ollie.

"No, I'm a boy and I live in a house with my Mommy and Daddy and my big brother."

"Do you live near here then Riley?"

"No, I am visiting my Grampy who lives just along the road."

Ollie says,

"I have a brother and three sisters, but they won't play with me because I am too little."

"Come on Riley dive under the water with me and we will go and chase some fish?"

"Don't be silly Ollie, I can't swim underwater and chase fish. They are much too fast for me."

"I can play with you up here if you want, do you like being splashed?"

"Oh yes Riley I love the water come on splash me, splash me."

"Hey that's fun Riley, I like this."

"It's getting late now, and my Mommy told me not to be out too long."

"Will you come back and play with me again one day?"

"I will if I can Ollie."
"Bye bye Ollie,"

"Bye bye Riley"

"Next time bring your big brother with you and we can all play together?"

"Perhaps I can get some of my brothers and sisters to come too," he added.

Riley grabbed his towel and ran back to his Grampy's house.

Oscar was sitting in the back garden reading a book when Riley came running in to tell him about Ollie.

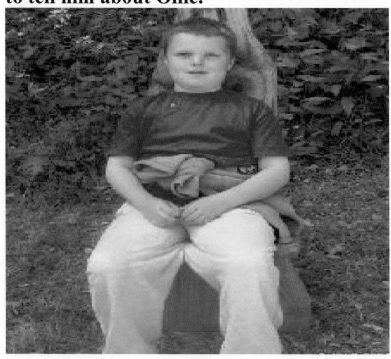

Oscar really wanted to read his book, but his younger brother was so excited about his new friend that he put his book down and listened to Riley.

"Oscar will you come with me tomorrow and we can both go and play with Ollie? He asked me to bring my brother so that we can all play together".

Oscar smiled and said,
"Otters can't talk, you are making this up".
"No, I am not," replied Riley.
"Just come with me and you will see."

"We must ask Mommy and Daddy," says Oscar.
"But don't mention that Ollie can talk," he added.

That evening after tea, Riley suddenly says to his Mommy,
"Can Oscar and I go and play down in the river tomorrow?"

Riley and Oscar are often squabbling and so it came as quite a surprise that the younger of the two boys asks that his brother go with him.

Mommy says quite loudly,

"How come you two want to play together?"

Riley was very quick to answer,
"I made friends with an Otter today and I wanted to take Oscar to see him," he said excitedly.

Their Mommy was intrigued but did not say no.

Daddy had gone down to the local newsagent to get the evening paper. It was about half a mile away and he enjoyed the walk down there. Grampy went with him which meant that they might be quite a long time because they would dawdle along and look in all the shop windows.

"Let's wait until tomorrow and we will see?" she replied.

She continued,

"Daddy and Grampy might have something else planned for tomorrow."

Riley looked a little bit disappointed but did not say anything else.

By the time Daddy and Grampy got home from the shops, the two boys were in the bathroom getting ready for bed.

Bed for a few days was a large couch downstairs in the sitting room. Grampy's cottage was exceedingly small and only had two bedrooms. The two boys thought it was fun sleeping on the couch.

Daddy waited downstairs until the boys were in their pyjamas and had come back down.

"Riley, Mommy tells me that you made a new friend today?" says Daddy.

"Yes Daddy, he is an otter and lives nearby somewhere on the river," replies Riley.

"Well, if you two boys want to stay and play with your new friend that should be alright but only until about four o'clock because we are going out for dinner tomorrow evening," says Daddy.

The two boys were very tired and were soon tucked up on the couch and sound asleep.

Riley was extremely excited and awoke early the following morning and gave his older brother a shove and told him to wake up.

Mommy had prepared breakfast, but they were almost too excited to stop and eat it.

Riley was in a hurry to take Oscar to meet his friend Ollie the Otter.

Daddy had gone to the front door to open it and let them out. Suddenly he shouted, "Come here boys, and look at this?"

"What are they Daddy?" asked Oscar. "Those are Canadian Geese and quite common in these parts," says Daddy.

"If they are Canadian, what are they doing here?" said Riley.

"Well, they are very common in many parts of the world and can fly very long distances," replied Daddy.

"Ooh look over there by the river there are some more geese with their babies" said a very excited Oscar.

Riley was getting a bit agitated now because he wanted to go and look for Ollie.

The two boys soon ran off down the road and very soon they were in the stream looking for Ollie.

"Are you sure he will come?" asks Oscar.
"He said he would, perhaps we should call
him," added Riley.

"Ollie, Ollie they shouted."

They were about to give up and go back to
the house when without any warning there
was a splash and a playful Ollie appeared

from under the water and remarkably close to them.

Oscar and Riley played with Ollie for several hours before they heard Mommy shouting for them to come in.

"We have to go now Ollie, it has been so much fun perhaps we can do it again one

day?" said Riley feeling a little sad that they had to go.
"Before you leave would you like to say hello to my brothers and sisters?" said Ollie.

"Where are they?" Asks Oscar.
"Right here," said a happy Ollie.

"Bye Bye Ollie, Bye Bye Ollie's family we have had a wonderful day,"

With that, Ollie and Ollie's family disappeared under the water and they were gone.

Mommy's voice came from up the road. "Come on boys time to get a bath and get ready to go out for dinner?"

"Alright", they both replied and scampered up the road to Grampy's house and the end of another adventure.

MY BOOKS: PAPERBACK AND KINDLE.

ALL AVAILABLE FROM AMAZON
amazon.com/author/garthtuxford

MY NOVELS
The Yemeni Effect
Regby Dornik - A Chilling Warning
Regby Dornik – The Fury of Inanna (sequel)
The Lion Hunter

CHILDREN'S BOOKS
Marti the Magnificent with Oscar and Riley (Age 5+)
Clive the Caterpillar with Oscar and Riley (Age 5+)
Ollie the Otter with Riley and Oscar (Age5+)
Marti the Meerkat with Oscar (Age 3+)
Lily, (The White Chihuahua) (Age 2+)

POETRY
Poetry Like No Other

CUISINE
Memaw's Recipes
International Quizine

PETS
Your Dog Ultimate Guide
Helpful Hints for Your Kitty

EXCERSISE
Walking for Weight Loss

DEDICATION

Judy and I married in 2014; we had previously been married and widowed and now both of us, in our late 70s, have embarked on a very exciting and fun new life.

Between us, we have a bunch of children, a bigger bunch of grandchildren, and are now at number seven on the great grandchildren list at the last count.

I would like to say a big thank you to Judy, who has put up with me and read every word I have written more times than I can remember.

We had fun with the spelling because I am English and she is American and I always like to say that the Americans love throwing letters out of words.

Thank you for your love and your encouragement – you were the driving force that got me to the end of all my books.

I have also written four novels, several children's books, and a book of 100 poems. Judy was there prodding me and constantly encouraging me to continue writing and to be the best that I could. Without her, I would not have succeeded.

Printed in Great Britain
by Amazon

33762881R00016